Story Co presents

The Ogre Bully

by A.B. Hoffmire

inspired by a folktale from Sweden

Long ago there was a little village in a country far away. In that little village there lived a young farmer and his family.

In those days almost everyone had to grow their own food. Each family had their own small farm.

The first day of spring the farmer went to work plowing his field.

At the very end of the very last row, he heard something strange. The grass rustled, trees swayed, and out of the woods stepped a big, gruff-looking ogre.

"What are you doing on my land?" demanded the ogre.

"Your land?" asked the farmer. "This is my family's field!"

"Oh really?" said the ogre. "Well I own this whole valley so I'll take the top part of any plants that you grow. Since I am so nice I'll let you keep the roots."

They argued for some time, but the ogre was very big and the farmer was not. In the end the ogre got his way.

The farmer did not like the ogre pushing him around. There would not be much to eat or sell with that ogre taking the top half of his crop.

"Don't worry," said his wife, who was very smart. "Since the ogre has left us the roots, plant a crop that grows underground... like carrots."

Well that is just what the farmer did.
He bought some carrot seeds and planted them.

Now carrots have tasty roots, but no one uses
the greens for anything.

The ogre, who was not very smart, did not
know that.

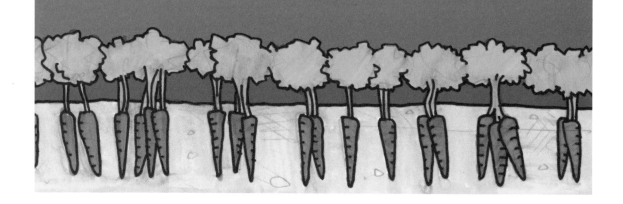

After the crops were picked, the ogre wanted to sell them at the market. The farmer had to pull the cart himself because his ox was afraid of the ogre.

At the market the farmer sold his carrots for a good price. Nobody wanted to buy the ogre's carrot greens.

On the way home the ogre complained. He did not like the way things turned out in the market.

"Look," said the ogre, "next time you take the top half, and I will take the roots."

"Okay," said the farmer. He knew what to do next.

This time the farmer planted tomatoes. When the plants were grown, they took them to the market. The farmer sold his tomatoes right away, but the ogre was stuck with the roots.

The ogre got angry and yelled, "From now on, I want the whole field!"

The ogr Got mad and said From now on I want the whole field.

"Since I am so nice," said the ogre, "I will give you one chance to keep your field." He challenged the farmer to a test of strength. They would see who could cut the grass the fastest. The winner would keep the whole field.

"I'll never be able to beat that huge ogre," moaned the farmer, but his wife had a plan.

The night before the race the farmer pulled the tomato stakes out of the ground in the part of the field he would cut.

The next day a crowd gathered to watch the contest. The farmer and the ogre prepared their tools. Everyone wanted to see who was the fastest. "I am so big and bad and strong!" the ogre roared to the crowd. The farmer looked scared.

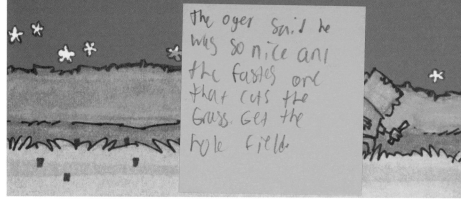

the oger said he was so nice and the fastes one that cuts the Grass. Get the hole field.

The race began. At first it was close. The ogre was very strong, and chopped through the stakes without feeling them. Soon the ogre's tool got beaten up, which slowed him down. The farmer started to pull ahead.

"Aren't you going to stop and sharpen your tool?" asked the ogre.

"Not yet," said the farmer.

"Forget it," said the ogre, "this farm work is too hard for me." To everyone's surprise he turned into a puff of smoke and drifted away in the wind.

When the ogre was gone the crowd cheered and everyone was happy that the farmer had won his field back.

Well, not everyone was happy. The ogre was
not happy at all. Still, it wasn't his field in the
first place so he didn't really lose anything.

The End